Postman Pat's
Holiday Packing

Story by John Cunliffe **Pictures by** Jane and Joan Hickson

from the original television designs by Ivor Wood

Scholastic Children's Books,
Commonwealth House, 1-19 New Oxford Street,
London WC1A 1NU, UK
a division of Scholastic Ltd
London ~ New York ~ Toronto ~ Sydney ~ Auckland
Mexico City ~ New Delhi ~ Hong Kong
First published by Scholastic Ltd, 1996
This edition published by Scholastic Ltd, 2000
Text copyright © John Cunliffe, 1996
Illustrations copyright © Scholastic Ltd and Woodland Animations Ltd, 1996
ISBN 0 439 99836 0

Printed in Singapore
The right of John Cunliffe, Joan Hickson and Ivor Wood to be identified as the
author and illustrators of this work respectively has been asserted by them in
accordance with the Copyright, Designs and Patents Act, 1988.

"I hate packing," said Pat.

"You have to do it," said Sara, "if you want to go on holiday, so stop grumbling. Come on, I'll help. First, pack your sponge-bag."

"Here it is," said Pat.

"Right," said Sara. "You'll need...your

toothbrush

toothpaste

razor

soap

face-cloth

and your comb.

That's six things."

"Right," said Pat.

"Best do it now," said Sara.

"In a minute," said Pat.

He stroked Jess, read the paper. Ate two sweets, and watered the plants.

Then he packed his sponge-bag.

"What did she say?" said Pat. "I'll need my...

soap

toothbrush

face-cloth

toothpaste

and my razor.

That's one...two...three...four...five...oh, there should be six! Now what have I missed?"

Sara was busy with her own packing now, so he didn't bother her. He sat a while and puzzled. At last, Pat said, "I know, I'll put some sweets in. You never know when we might be hungry."

"Did you put six things in your sponge-bag?" said Sara.

"Yes," said Pat.

"Good. Now get the suitcases out."

Pat got the suitcases from the loft.
Sara opened the wardrobe.

"Now," she said, "you'll need your...

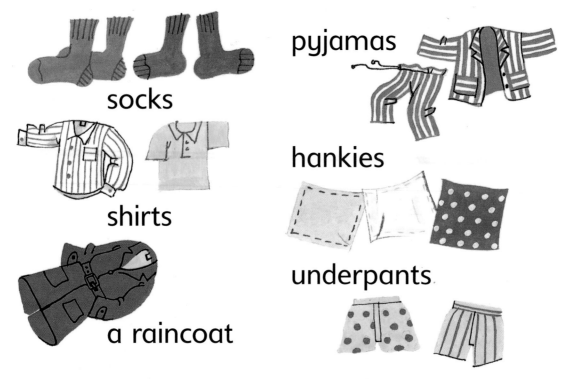

socks

pyjamas

shirts

hankies

a raincoat

underpants

and anything else you can think of. That's six
more things you must not forget."

"Right," said Pat.

He polished his shoes, stroked Jess again, had a drink of water, and went to the toilet.

Then he packed his suitcase.

"Another six things," he said. "Let's see, now...

one – pyjamas

two – underpants

three – shirts

four – socks

five – hankies

six – er...ummm...what can it be? Well, any number of things."

17

Pat put lots more things in his case.
He counted them in...

"Six – a radio,

seven – some biscuits,

eight – a book,

nine – a game,

ten – more sweets,

eleven – slippers,

and twelve – a sun-hat.

"Twelve things," he said. "There can't be anything missing. Besides, my case is full."

"Have you finished?" said Sara.

"Yes," said Pat.

"Good," said Sara. "Did you put six things in?"

"Six and six again," said Pat.

"Come and help me with mine," said Sara.

Pat lost count of all the things that Sara packed. She sent him all over the house collecting things; dresses and skirts, and stockings, and knickers, and lipsticks, and blouses; a raincoat; an umbrella; three pairs of shoes; slippers; three scarves; a jumper and a woolly; and so much more. She filled three cases, two bags, and a rucksack.

"Is that it?" said Pat.

"I think so," said Sara. "I hope I haven't forgotten anything."

"What about the bath?" said Pat. "And the cooker?"

"Don't be silly," said Sara. "I hope *you* didn't forget anything!"

"I don't think so," said Pat. "I put lots of things in. Look, my case is full."

"It'll do," said Sara. "I'm too tired with all my packing to check on yours."

On the last day of their holiday, Sara said, "Best get your raincoat out. I think it's going to rain today."

"That's a good idea," said Pat. "Now, then, raincoat...let's see, now where did I put it...hmmmm...raincoat...raincoat...now where..."

He tipped his case out on the bed. He spread out all the things he had packed. There was no raincoat.

"You've forgotten it," said Sara, "and mine won't fit you."

"Never mind," said Pat, "it might not rain."

It didn't. Well, not until Pat and Sara were miles away, with no shelter at all. Then it poured. Poor Pat. He was soaked!

29

When they got back to the hotel, Pat had to go to bed whilst his clothes dried. Sara went to a film. When she came back, Pat's clothes were nearly dry. She said, "That's the best film I've ever seen!"

"Never mind," said Pat. "I found a book in my case, and read that. It was so good that I forgot all about my wet clothes."

"We'd better dry your clothes before morning," said Sara. "You cannot go on the train in your pyjamas."

After that, whenever they went on holiday, Pat always took a raincoat, *and* a good book. Just in case.